DONALD and DOUGLAS

Based on *The Railway Series* by the Rev. W. Awdry

Illustrations by
Robin Davies and Creative Design

EGMONT

EGMONT

We bring stories to life

First published in Great Britain in 2003
by Egmont UK Limited
239 Kensington High Street, London W8 6SA
This edition published in 2008
All Rights Reserved

HiT entertainment

ISBN 978 1 4052 3449 8

1 3 5 7 9 10 8 6 4 2

Printed in Italy

The Forest Stewardship Council (FSC) is an international, non-governmental organisation dedicated to promoting responsible management of the world's forests. FSC operates a system of forest certification and product labelling that allows consumers to identify wood and wood-based products from well managed forests.

For more information about Egmont's paper buying policy please visit www.egmont.co.uk/ethicalpublishing

For more information about the FSC please visit their website at www.fsc.uk.org

But the next day, The Fat Controller got a surprise. Not one, but two engines arrived from Scotland! They were twins called Donald and Douglas, and they had lost their numbers. No one knew which of them was supposed to stay!

"One of you will have to go back to Scotland," said The Fat Controller. "I will paint numbers on you for now, but I will decide which is the better engine, and send the other one home."

So the engines were given new numbers. Donald was number nine and Douglas was number ten.

Donald and Douglas felt miserable. Neither of them wanted to stay without the other.

"We'll just have to be so well-behaved that he'll want to keep us both!" said Douglas.

"Aye!" said Donald. "He won't be able to choose between us!"

The twins enjoyed working on The Fat Controller's Railway. They were good at keeping the trucks in order, and they soon made friends with the other engines.

Every day, Gordon's express train steamed in with a special coach for passengers travelling on Thomas' branch line. Duck had to remember to shunt the special coach for Thomas to pick up.

Douglas said to Duck, "Why don't I move the special coach tomorrow?"

"That would be very kind, Douglas," said Duck, gratefully.

The next day, when Gordon arrived with the special coach, Douglas was busy worrying about being sent back to Scotland.

"I couldn't abide going back alone," said Douglas to himself.

He was so worried that he forgot to take the special coach to Thomas. He pushed it into the siding and went to join Donald.

When Thomas came along, he couldn't find his coach. A group of angry passengers complained to The Fat Controller. The Fat Controller went to find Douglas.

"I'm very annoyed, Douglas," he said. "It looks as though you may be going back to Scotland!"

Next day, Douglas was extra careful and he didn't do anything wrong. But Donald was unlucky. He backed into a siding where the rails were slippery. Poor Donald couldn't stop! He crashed through the buffers into a signal box, leaving the Signalman sitting on the coal in the tender!

"You clumsy great engine!" cried the Signalman. "You've jammed my points!"

The Fat Controller was very annoyed.
"I'm disappointed in you, Donald," he said.
"I was going to send Douglas back and keep you, but now I'm not so sure!"

Donald felt very sorry.

That night, snow came to the island and covered all the tracks. Most engines hate snow, but Donald and Douglas loved it! They knew just what to do. They puffed busily backwards and forwards, patrolling the line. They even rescued other engines who got stuck in the snow-drifts.

All the other engines liked Donald and Douglas. Everyone was sad that one of them was going to be sent away.

"They were wonderful in the snow," said Henry.

"What we need is a Deputation," said Edward.

"What is a Depotstation?" asked Henry.

"A Deputation is when engines tell The Fat Controller that something is wrong, and ask him to put it right," replied Edward.

"I propose," said Gordon quickly, "that Percy be our Desperation."

So it was Percy's job to speak to The Fat Controller. He wished it wasn't!

"Please, Sir, they've made me a Disputation," said Percy. "To speak to you, Sir."

"Do you mean a Deputation?" asked The Fat Controller.

"Yes, Sir. It's Donald and Douglas, Sir. Please don't send them away, Sir. They're nice engines, Sir."

The Fat Controller smiled.

The next day, The Fat Controller went to see Donald and Douglas.

"I hear you have been doing good work in the snow. What colour paint would you like?"

The twin engines stared at him.
"Blue please, Sir," they said in surprise.
"Does this mean … we'll both be staying, Sir?" asked Donald.

"It certainly does!" said The Fat Controller. But the rest of his speech was drowned in a delighted chorus of cheers and whistles!

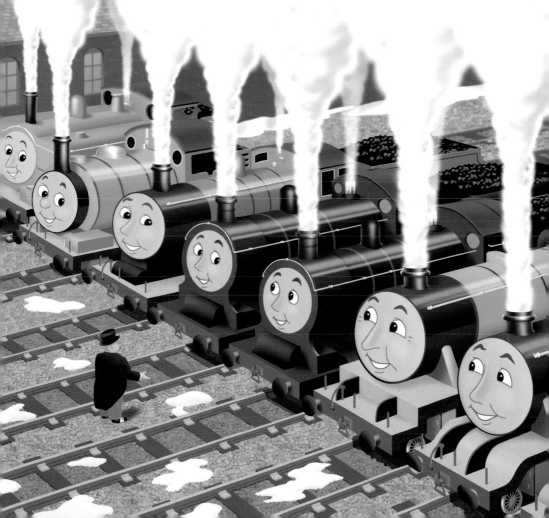

The Thomas Story Library is THE definitive collection of stories about Thomas and ALL his friends.

5 more Thomas Story Library titles will be chuffing into your local bookshop in August 2008!

Jeremy
Hector
BoCo
Billy
Whiff

And there are even more Thomas Story Library books to follow later

So go on, start your Thomas Story Library NOW!

A Fantastic Offer for Thomas the Tank Engine Fans!

STICK POUND COIN HERE

In every Thomas Story Library book like this one, you will find a special token. Collect 6 Thomas tokens and we will send you a brilliant Thomas poster, and a double-sided bedroom door hanger! Simply tape a £1 coin in the space above, and fill out the form overleaf.

TO BE COMPLETED BY AN ADULT

To apply for this great offer, ask an adult to complete the coupon below
and send it with a pound coin and 6 tokens, to:
THOMAS OFFERS, PO BOX 715, HORSHAM RH12 5WG

☐ Please send a Thomas poster and door hanger. I enclose 6 tokens
plus a £1 coin. (Price includes P&P)

Fan's name...

Address...

....Postcode..........................

Date of birth...

Name of parent/guardian..

Signature of parent/guardian...

Please allow 28 days for delivery. Offer is only available while stocks last. We reserve the right to change
the terms of this offer at any time and we offer a 14 day money back guarantee. This does not affect your
statutory rights.

☐ Data Protection Act: If you do not wish to receive other similar offers from us or companies we
recommend, please tick this box. Offers apply to UK only.

Cut along the dotted line